Parental Guide to Bedtime Stories from the Barn

Beverly A. Stubblefield, Ph.D.

To order additional copies of this book, contact:
Xlibris
844-714-8691
www.Xlibris.com
Orders@Xlibris.com

ISBN: Softcover   978-1-6698-2933-1
         EBook   978-1-6698-2932-4

Print information available on the last page

Rev. date: 07/06/2022

CONTENTS

"Train up a child in the way that he should go and even when he is old, he will not depart from it." (Proverbs 22:6)

This Parental Guide is a companion to *Bedtime Stories from the Barn,* which is designed to help parents and caretakers teach children the understanding of basic psychological principles found in God's Word through the metaphor of the horses' conversations. As with the Proverbs of King Solomon, the purpose of the Parental Guide is to teach wisdom, discipline, and provide insights that will help children live successful lives by discerning and doing what is right, just, and fair according to God's Word (Proverbs 1:1-4).

Parents are to read the bedtime stories, listen to the children's comments and questions, explore the true meaning of the stories, and provide understanding and guidance. In addition to Scripture references, psychological principles and techniques are provided in this guide to help parents and children learn effective coping skills to deal with today's issues. And if the children's questions get too difficult, don't be afraid to ask for help! A glossary of "horse" words is included to better understand the horses' world depicted in the bedtime stories.

This Parental Guide is also a helpful resource family therapists can recommend to their clients to facilitate the therapeutic process at home.

"I am teaching you today—yes, you—so you will trust in the Lord" (Proverbs 22:19).

"Commit yourself to instruction, listen carefully to words of knowledge" (Proverbs 23:12).

". . . Promote the kind of living that reflects wholesome teachings" (Titus 2:1).

ANGER MANAGEMENT

To accompany the Bedtime Stories

ANGER and COMPETITION

"Provoke not your children to wrath: but bring them up in the nurture and admonition of the Lord." (Ephesians 6:4 KJV)

Anger and frustration are normal feelings. How we manage them is important. In the Bedtime Story "Competition", Chad and Smokey respected and loved each other. But under the stress and pressure of a horse show, Chad became aggravated and wasn't his typically easy-going self. He became frustrated by not placing in any of the classes. He wanted to blame Smokey, but it was his angry jerking of the horse that the judge saw and caused him not to place. Chad learned that getting angry and frustrated didn't improve one's performance.

From the horse's perspective, Smokey was hurt physically and emotionally by Chad's jerking. Chad's behavior confused Smokey. After cooling down and reflecting about the show on the ride home, Chad realized that he needed to apologize to Smokey. After unloading, grooming, and feeding Smokey, Chad lovingly put his arms around him and apologized. Chad reassured Smokey of their relationship, which strengthened their bond.

As a parent, it is important to maintain your calm even when angered. As an adult, you are to be an example of anger management and appropriate behavior. Don't back yourself into a corner by making harsh demands or idle threats like,"I'm going to kill you when we get home", something you know you will never do—but something that will intimidate and strike fear in your child. This is a poor strategy.

All-or-nothing thinking can lead to this dysfunctional parenting style.

Blaming negatively affects your child's self-esteem. When a parent tries to be powerful instead of loving, the child typically responds with rebellion, more anger, and if chronic—eventually to violence (the kick the dog syndrome: Boss yells at employee, employee goes home and yells at wife, wife yells at child, child kicks the dog). Allow yourself and your child time and space to calm down and outline more effective consequences. Time-out is effective in accomplishing this. (One minute per child's age.)

Stop and think—don't react. It was the overreaction and loss of control by the rider in the bedtime story "Anger" that caused her to lose first place. Practice calming statements and self-talk strategies for maintaining control (Novacco). For example, "My feelings are a cue to cope. Just relax, take a deep breath, count to ten." If only the rider in "Anger" had not blamed her horse and had thought about the consequences of her actions before striking her horse. Maybe she would have won first place after all.

Try to see things from your child's perspective. Choose consequences in relation to the child's age and stage of development. Don't "gunny sack", that is, don't save up all of your frustrations and dump them all at once. If you lose your temper, apologize, but don't react out of guilt. Ask for and accept forgiveness. Reassure your child that your upset is not at them as a person but by the events at hand. Remember, you are the role model for your child. Be how you want your children to become.

"Do not seek revenge or bear a grudge . . . but love your neighbor as yourself." (Leviticus 19:18).

This goes for your children and animals as well.

"Be angry and sin not; let not the sun go down upon your wrath." (Ephesians 4:26).

DEPRESSION

To accompany the Bedtime Stories

CAMP BEARABLE and TRUST

Typically, children do not exhibit depression like adults do—they do not have the cognitive constructs to understand or express what they are feeling. Depressed children typically exhibit frustration, irritability, and anger as opposed to sadness, crying spells, sleep and appetite disturbance, etc. in adults.

How do I know if my child is depressed? If there is no specific antecedent for their behavior, that is, if you can't pinpoint a real reason for their behavior, then observe, talk, and listen to your child. You may have to give them the words to describe their feelings. Hopefully, that's what the horses do in the bedtime stories from the barn. Find out what your child's behavior is like at school. Is your child being bullied, is there a learning deficit, can they see and hear what is going on in the classroom, or is there a problem for which they may be being teased?

In more extreme forms of depression, your child may exhibit decreased appetite, sleep disturbance, and social withdrawal. Withdrawal was one of the ways the horse, Caio, coped with his depression in the Bedtime Story "Trust". His behavior made the other horses think he was conceited or "stuck up" because of his special breeding and training. But that was not the case. Caio was depressed. The same is true with people. Many depressed individuals are labeled as conceited when they are socially withdrawn due to feelings of depression.

What to do—spend more quality time with your child. That is what the Bedtime Stories are all about. Ask questions and LISTEN. When Caio got to live on a cattle ranch again, his depression lifted. Get to know your child as an individual separate from you. Allow your child to be as God created him or her. Respect their interests and their character. Not everyone is cut out to play football or be a ballerina.

Model good coping skills. This means you, too, Dad and grandparents. Let your child know that you've felt the same way they are feeling or have had a similar experience to theirs and tell them how you coped or wish you had coped better. Hopefully, they can learn from our mistakes. Don't be like the Dad in "Leading From Behind" and bark orders while doing nothing. That is ineffective role modeling.

Sometimes childhood bipolar disorder is misdiagnosed as attention deficit/hyperactivity disorder. Bipolar kids show mood swings, sleep and appetite problems (often diagnosed as a picky eater), but often they typically self-medicate with sugar like bipolar adults do with alcohol and are mislabeled as alcoholics—a symptom of a deeper problem.

If your child's depression lasts weeks and months, see a child psychologist first for an appropriate diagnosis before seeking medication. Check their diet and consult a dietitian for foods that stimulate neurochemicals naturally. Engage your child in physical activity to stimulate endorphins. Reduce stressors, BE with them (color, play ball, have a tea party), reduce time with electronics, encourage play outdoors with other kids. Don't schedule them to death. Allow your child to be a kid. Use your imagination and encourage them to use theirs.

Love them. Give your children hugs and kisses, but don't try to buy their love. Boost their self-esteem by stating positives about them daily, like the maid did in the movie THE HELP—"you are smart, you are beautiful, you are loved." Catch them doing something good instead of always looking at what they are doing wrong. Remind them of God's love and how He sees us. Give them hope!

If your children get too discouraged, they won't listen; they'll just give up and become hopeless and apathetic, just like the Israelites didn't listen to Moses because they had been beaten down so much by Pharaoh. They regressed when he was out of sight as children often do when parents are away.

Don't stress them out by placing too many demands on them or by over scheduling them. Sometimes we place unrealistic expectations on our children. We expect them to be "mini me's" and take up where we left off in sports, academics, etc. Accept each child as a separate individual with different interests, thoughts, and abilities. Sometimes our expectations can be very innocent like the time my father had the grandchildren help him rake the yard. He can last forever outside, but the grandchildren were not used to his work ethic. My father asked John to perform some adult task and John responded with "but Granddaddy, I'm only ten years old." Granddaddy then realized he had unrealistic expectations of John's physical abilities.

Be Positive. Look at the glass of water as half full instead of half empty. Start each day with a positive. My father used to wake us up each morning by flipping on the light switch and quoting Isaiah 60:1 KJV: "Arise, shine; for thy light is come, and the glory of the Lord is risen upon thee." We weren't happy about the light coming on, but his words about the glory of the Lord got us up without grumbling. Give your child at least three positive's daily, like taking medicine three times a day. This reinforces positive self-esteem and self-worth. Even when you need to discipline your child, start with a positive like, "Thank you for coloring a picture for me, but please color on the paper, not the furniture next time." Then have the child help you clean the mess.

Teach them. Engage your child in household tasks and activities with you to teach them about the practical things in life. Give them a dust cloth to wipe furniture after you've applied the polish. Have them accompany you to the hardware store to purchase parts to repair the lawnmower. Have them read a recipe to you while you cook. Show them how to properly use tools like screwdrivers. My sister and I destroyed many kitchen knives trying to screw the drawer pull on our dresser.

Each of the above suggestions will help your child develop a positive attitude and improve self-esteem which will help thwart depression.

LISTEN

To accompany the Bedtime Stories

A NEW TRAINER and THE COWBOY

Communication is essential in establishing a relationship, whether it be between horse and rider or parent and child. Just like the horses learned to listen to help boys and girls in the story "The Beginning", parents need to learn to listen. Communication involves both speaking and listening. To get someone to listen to you, even a horse, you must first get their attention. Horse trainers use many different "cues" but the most important one is their physical presence in the horse pen. And that is the best way to get your child's attention—be physically present with them, not yelling from the other room, like my mother used to do. It was so easy to ignore her and pretend we didn't hear her. In the story "Leading From Behind", the father's telling everyone what to do and barking orders but doing nothing himself only led to confusion and upset feelings.

Show compassion: Once your child starts talking, don't interrupt or correct them or their speech. Employ active listening to get to the root of the problem and to show them you understand and are not judgmental. Allow them to complain as Job did, "Don't simply condemn me" (Job 10:2). "If you listen, I will show you. I will answer you from my own experience" (Job 15:17). ". . . but you don't listen because you don't belong to God" (John 8:47b). ". . . as a loincloth clings to a man's waist, so I created Judah and Israel to cling to me says the Lord. They were to be my people, my pride, my glory—an honor to my name. But they would not listen to me" (Jeremiah 13:11).

In the story "Forgiveness", Jack got hurt because he didn't listen to Aunt Bev telling him to stop kicking Apache. Just like parents want their children to listen to them for instruction to keep them "safe", God –our Heavenly Father—wants us to listen to Him to keep us safe from sin and its consequences. But as the verses above show, both in the Old Testament, the New Testament, and today, we don't listen. God and Jesus and the Holy Spirit speak to us from a position of love and compassion to establish and maintain boundaries of right living just like a good parent. Blessings occur within those boundaries (Tony Evans). The best way to get your children to listen to you is to model listening to them. Here are some helpful ways to actively listen:

Active Listening

Listening is an active, not a passive process. To employ active listening skills, follow these simple steps:

A. *Turn yourself off and tune in your child*, much like a radio receiver. Don't worry about what to say. Your child will provide the necessary words.

B. Use one of these four techniques to show that you are listening:

   1. *Reflecting*—just as a mirror reflects what is before it, reflect by repeating verbatim what your child says. For example, if your child says "I'm afraid," you say "you're afraid?"

   2. *Paraphrasing*— is similar to reflecting. Repeat what is said but use your own words. For example, "I'm afraid" becomes "you're scared?"

   3. *Drawing out*—get your child to expound on what is said by stating, "tell me more about it" or by asking a direct question—"who, what, when, where, why, how?"

   4. *Clarification*—this is probably the best technique to use to let the other person know they've been heard. Use phrases such as "I understand you to say . . .", "what I hear you saying is . . .", or by simply restating the facts as presented by the other person.

C. *Don't argue*; simply restate what you've heard.

D. *Nonverbal communication* is just as powerful as verbal communication. The adage "A picture is worth a thousand words" best sums up this concept. Use appropriate nonverbal skills when listening and speaking with your child, such as the following:

   1. *Eye contact*—look the other person in the eye but don't make them uncomfortable. When communicating with another person, look at their nose, eyebrows, hairline, anywhere in the direction of their face.

   2. *Facial expression*—Sometimes our facial expression may send an incorrect message, like in "The Cows" and "Cell Phone", JR and Skeeter were afraid

that Aunt Bev was angry. Instead, she was just upset. Have expression on your face that matches the feeling being stated. For example, you would not smile while stating, "I'm so sorry your fish died" nor would you grimace while stating, "this won't hurt you a bit." Your child can tell whether you are lying or telling the truth by the expression on your face.

3. *Voice tone, inflection, and volume*—just as your facial expression tells a story, so does your voice; therefore, your tone should match what you are saying. Don't yell or speak too harshly but speak audibly and firmly when you need to get your child's attention. Use some "sparkle" in your voice instead of a constant monotone. This will keep your child's attention during the story or anytime you want your child to listen. As you read the Bedtime Stories, animate your voice when speaking for the horses.

4. *Use gestures*, such as head nods, appropriate hand motions, etc., to emphasize a point. This also helps to maintain your child's attention.

5. *Body posture*—I'm not talking about sitting up straight, although this does help to maintain attention and improve listening. I'm talking about maintaining a body position that faces the other person so that you can maintain eye contact and they can easily see your facial expression. Face-to-face communication is usually better than side-by-side communication; however, for the Bedtime Stories, you will likely want to sit beside your child in bed with your arm around them as they help hold the story book. Lean forward or toward the child when making a point but maintain appropriate personal space.

6. *Timing*—speak when spoken to. Timing is a critical nonverbal cue in communication. Sometimes silence is appropriate; however, at other times, silence may convey an inappropriate response. Silence may be viewed as a lack of caring. Silence may also promote anxiety in your child. The silent treatment is often harsh. Therefore, make a statement such as "let me think about that", or "I don't know" instead of not responding. The worst punishment I ever received was my father not talking to me after being caught driving the car where I wasn't supposed to go. I kept waiting for him to levy punishment, but he never did. The anxiety I put upon myself was enough punishment. As a result, I never drove the car down that road again.

"Open our ears Lord, may we hear and listen to your Word. Listening means application of your instruction! Thank you dear Heavenly Father that I have ears to hear. Now may I listen to stay within the path—boundaries—that you have set forth for my life." So, as the horses did in the story "Listen", just "listen".

ANXIETY, FEAR, AND PHOBIAS

To accompany the Bedtime Stories

CONFRONTING FEAR, CELL PHONE, THE BEGINNING, THE WILD
BOAR, MIDNIGHT TRAIL RIDE, THE COWS, THE PARADE, THE TURTLE,
THE OBSTACLE COURSE, ENTANGLED, THE FIRE, THE SHADOWS

"The Lord is my light and my salvation, so why should I be afraid?
The Lord is my fortress, protecting me from danger, so why should
I tremble? . . . I will remain confident" (Psalm 27:1 & 3).

Fear of the unknown and unfamiliar, like JR in the story "The Cows", is the most common type of anxiety. JR had never been around cows before and he didn't know what to think about those different creatures. After carefully allowing JR to become accustomed to the cows, Aunt Bev reminded JR to "be of good courage and fear not" (Joshua 1:6-9). In the story "Confronting Fear", Terry felt fear when he first got on the horse Dude because it was a totally new experience for him. Aunt Bev was anxious about showing JR in a different arena in the story "Competition". All too often our fear and worry is for nothing. In the story "Cell Phone", after he accidentally stepped on the cell phone, Roanie reassured Skeeter, "Don't worry; your fear is for nothing. Stepping on the cell phone was an accident, and Aunt Bev and Nancy know you didn't mean to step on it."

As with the loss of the use of the cell phone, most anxiety is about some type of loss: loss of emotional security as when a second child arrives; feelings of abandonment when parents take a trip and kids are left with grandparents for two weeks; separation from secure, good-enough parents due to illness, work, etc.; death of a beloved pet; relocation to a new home, like Mongo and Clyde in the story "Rescued Horses"; losing a toy; even normal everyday activities that may suddenly change or new activities never before experienced can produce anxiety.

For example: When my brother was about seven years old, our family went to Miami. We traveled in a yellow 1965 Ford Falcon that had no air-conditioning. Somewhere along the way, the car lost its muffler (there's the loss). As a result, the car made a loud noise, sputtered and smoked, but otherwise ran efficiently. My brother, however, began to worry about running out of gas. He literally worried himself sick to the point of running a temperature and throwing up (the excessive carbon-dioxide fumes may have had something to do with it). A doctor was called to our hotel to examine my brother. He found nothing seriously wrong and pronounced the diagnosis as anxiety. Reassured by the doctor, then by my father, my brother was able to relax and enjoy the trip. (The muffler was repaired for the return trip home). "I prayed to the Lord and He answered me. He freed me from all my fears" (Psalm 34:4).

We never know what may be troubling our children, but our response to daily activities can make or break their sense of security. For example: When I was in the eighth grade, my family went to the Mid-south Fair in Memphis (where Elvis Presley got his start). The Fair's signature ride was the Pippin Roller Coaster. Rather reluctantly, I convinced my father to ride it with me. After the first hill, I began screaming, "Daddy, Daddy, make it stop!" Now, I was in the eighth grade and logically I knew there was nothing Daddy could do. But instead of calmly reassuring me that I was safe and the ride would be over soon, Daddy said nothing. I glanced over at my father who was holding on for dear life himself, and I realized that he was just as scared as I was. THAT was the trauma—not so much the ride—but seeing my father, my hero, being afraid of something. The reality of Daddy's humanity shook my idealization of him. Well, I never rode the Pippin or any other carnival ride after that except for kiddy rides like the merry-go-round. I developed a phobia. It wasn't worth treating at the time because I rarely went to fairs or carnivals. But it did pose a problem when I was in high school and dating. I stood on the sideline and held the purses while my friends rode the rides.

In graduate school after studying systematic desensitization, I began to work on overcoming my phobia. Gradually, I started riding more and more adventurous carnival rides until I was finally able to ride the Pippin without fear. I walked away smiling. Years later, I remembered my success and rode every ride at Opryland with my sister, niece, and nephew. They never knew I ever had a phobia to carnival rides. I remained calm and positive.

Just like me and Terry in "Confronting Fear", learning to relax and thinking positively is important for parents to learn, teach, and practice. The following are some important techniques to learn and use:

Diaphragmic Breathing: It was diaphragmic breathing that Terry used to help him stay calm and ride Dude in the story "Confronting Fear". Singing engages our diaphragm and helps us stay calm. Use imagery of calming places such as the beach or the mountains to teach this very effective technique to your children. Terry thought of himself as a cowboy at "Home on the Range." Clear your mind of all thoughts by imagining a little man inside your head with a big bucket of white paint, whiting out the inside of your mind so that you can concentrate on your breathing. Begin to take slow, deep, even breaths by inhaling through your nose, holding your breath a few seconds, and then exhaling through your mouth. Counting can help to accomplish this. Inhale to a count of four, hold your breath to a count of four, then, exhale to a count of eight. Imagine that you are breathing in sunshine and freshness and exhaling darkness, danger, etc. Then project your calming scene onto the blank screen in your mind or see yourself accomplishing a task, such as making a homerun or a strike in bowling. This is the technique Aunt Bev used to remain calm in the story "The Parade", which also helped JR calm down. As JR said, "I know Aunt Bev loves us and protects us even when we are afraid."

Thought Stopping: If you find yourself ruminating about negative events, yell "STOP!" to yourself. Clear your mind; begin to think positively. You may have to momentarily change your activity or position to accomplish this. Sometimes you might have to yell "STOP!" out loud. When I was single, living in South Carolina, I was very lonely and on the verge of depression. I did not like my new job and I missed my friends, especially on Sunday afternoons. To cope, I started going outside and walking by the lake in the beautiful mountains to distract my dysfunctional thinking. And it lifted my spirit.

Positive thinking: Focus on the facts, not the "what if's". Look around and find something positive to focus on (like the lake and mountains around me in South Carolina). Describe it to your child. It could be as big as a sunset or as small as their toes. Quoting comforting, meaningful scripture verses is another way to refocus negative thinking.

Shaping: Reward successive approximations to the goal. This process involves rewarding behaviors that may initially only faintly resemble the desired behavioral goal. Break down an activity or event into smaller steps. Begin with the easiest first—don't go jumping off the deep end! This technique helps to reduce fear of major tasks, like swimming, riding a bike, etc. Gradually practice and reward each step until it is accomplished successfully, and then move on to the next step until the goal is accomplished. This technique is used to train horses. It may take awhile, but it helps establish a healthy relationship built on trust when done correctly. Rewarding successive approximations to the goal helps to eliminate intimidation. Watch some horse training videos to see what I am talking about. In teaching the campers to ride, we began by leading them on the horse. Then they rode at a walk, next at a trot, finally at a lope but never at a gallop. KEEP YOUR CHILDREN SAFE. If your child doesn't like a particular activity, don't force it. Figure some way to make it more fun for them if it is something they—not you—really want to do. That was my experience with our grandson Georgie. Both sides of the family had been heavily involved in showing horses, even his mom. But Georgie didn't grow up going to the barn every day. And when his beautiful Paso Fino, Julio, ran away with him (actually he just trotted off), Georgie became fearful of riding. You see, we exposed him too fast, not recognizing his unfamiliarity with horses. He didn't really understand what "pull back on the reins" meant. What helped Georgie become an accomplished rider was having him help me with the therapeutic riding group. One day I asked him to ride with another fearful child to model that it was okay. And Georgie did. Now he rides JR all by himself comfortably at a trot. We needed to give Georgie time and space. He needed that time to learn to trust the horses and us.

Modeling: Children imitate us whether we like it or not. In the story "The Missing Saddle", Aunt Bev's nervousness and feelings of frustration led Roanie to feel anxious. We adults, especially parents and caretakers, need to be mindful of our own behavior around children and animals as well. In the story "Cell Phone", Skeeter recognized Nancy's anxiety but remained calm. Again, behave like you want your children to behave. They will act out what they see and hear. Talk like you want them to talk, do what you want them to do, eat what you want them to eat, etc. So who should we as parents imitate? "Imitate God!" (Ephesians 5:1): "Live a life filled with love, following the example of Christ."

Praise your children when they model good behavior. Just like the Cowboy, Mr. Harold, did in training Panda, reward successive approximations to the goal to shape a desired behavior. That means to praise or give small treats for behaviors that are close to the desired end result. You don't wait until a child hits a homerun to praise them. Praise and give encouragement all along the way. That's what the "New Trainer" did in the story about training Apache. She patted his withers whenever he correctly followed her command, which wasn't very often, unfortunately.

Provide reassurance: Wise old Skeeter was good at providing reassurance, especially in the story "Midnight Trail Ride". He reassured the horses by quoting scripture verses: "Be strong and courageous. Do not be afraid or discouraged for the Lord is with you wherever you go" (Joshua 1:6-9). Teaching your children reassuring scripture verses is another way of providing internalization.

Be trustworthy: Sometimes our children fear the consequences of their behavior, even if it is an accident, just like Skeeter did in the story "Cell Phone". Children need to have confidence that parents will take care of them and meet their needs, just like the horses knew that Aunt Bev would care for them and do nothing to harm them intentionally. Don't bully your children. Do what you say you are going to do. Meet your child's basic needs. Then they can trust and feel secure. When children feel secure, they feel loved and they show love in return. In the story "The Shadows", JR states, "I had to learn to trust Aunt Bev to keep me safe. Aunt Bev would never put us in danger on purpose." As quoted in the story "A Winter's Night", Matthew 6:25 tells us not to worry. "Your Heavenly Father already knows all your needs and He will give you everything you need." That's great reassurance! All we have to do is trust.

Use calming imagery: What is calming imagery? Wise old Skeeter said it best in the story "Test Anxiety", "That means you are supposed to relax and imagine yourself remaining calm and completing activities successfully whenever you are in a challenging situation." In addition to diaphragmic breathing, Gail used calming imagery to visualize positive results in the story "Test Anxiety". Teach your children to visualize performing an activity successfully, such as hitting the baseball, throwing a strike in bowling, remaining in the saddle, etc. Then have them perform the activity slowly but surely.

Pray instead of worrying as Aunt Bev did when Prince was missing in the story "Entangled". There will be many anxious moments rearing children, but prayer and meditation help calm frazzled nerves. Start the day with prayer for yourself and your family. End the day with bedtime prayers after reading a story. Pray throughout the day for leadership and wise discernment in the challenges that come your way, like Aunt Bev did in the story "Competition". "Pray without ceasing" (1 Thessalonians 5:17). Teach your children to pray to help reduce their own anxieties. This is what my nephew Chad did whenever he had a test at school. In the story "The Cows", JR prayed thanking God for calming his fears and asked Him to bless the horses with a good night's sleep." As JR learned, "Quoting Bible verses and believing in positive outcomes is the answer for most of our problems, especially our fears."

ABANDONMENT

To accompany the Bedtime Stories

THE MARE AND THE COLT and GENTLE SPIRIT

"Do not turn your back on me. Do not reject your servant in anger . . .
Don't leave me now, don't abandon me. Even if my father and mother
abandon me, the Lord will hold me close" (Psalm 27:9-10).

The mare Shiloh and her colt Apache could not be separated without Apache becoming wild. When Shiloh heard Apache's "cries" for her, she became unruly, paced, and was uncontrollable until Apache was in her sight again. Unlike Shiloh and Apache, the horse Dillon showed no feelings of abandonment when he left his original home to come to The Equestrian Therapy Center. He had a healthy, internalized attachment to a little girl in the story "Gentle Spirit". He was thus able to form good attachments to other horses and people. Dillon remembered the little girl and she remembered him.

The psychological process of internalization must occur in an individual to prevent feelings of abandonment. To internalize means to make other people's behaviors, beliefs, or ideas (especially the prevailing society's attitudes, mores, norms, etc.) as a part of one's own thinking and behavior. A first step in the internalization process is the development of object constancy. Object constancy is when we know an object or person exists even though we don't see them. In the game of "peep eye", infants younger than six months are always surprised to see the face of a person behind hands held to the face when they are removed. They don't know that objects or people still exist when they are not seen. After six months of age or so, children know to remove the hands to reveal the hidden face because they have developed object constancy. They know the person still exists hidden behind the hands.

It is through the process of internalization that we learn the rules of safety: look both ways before crossing the street, hot—don't touch, don't spit, don't hit, and don't chew with your mouth full. Children come to unconsciously follow internalized rules and rituals because they have been repeated to them so often.

The concept of internalization is important in Christianity. Through the power of the Holy Spirit, Christ is internalized in those who believe. This is why the Holy Spirit is known as "the Comforter". We will never be forgotten or forsaken. It is important for children to know this and internalize the Word of God by memorizing scripture. It is important for parents and caretakers to model the peace of mind that comes with the internalization of the Holy Spirit.

Apache had always been with his mother so he had no need to internalize her. He didn't have to leave to go to school or get training like our children do. However, as a result, he was unable to be away from her presence or out of her sight. He was anxious and insecure without her. That made him dangerous.

Apache had to change his perception about being away from his mother. He had to internalize another being, and that's what Skeeter talked with him about in the story "The Mare and the Colt". Apache was able to internalize the fact that God was with him wherever he went and that He would never abandon him. In the story "A New Trainer", Apache remembered what Skeeter had told him about God, "I will never fail you. I will never abandon you" (Hebrews 13:5). Apache was eventually able to remain separated from Shiloh, but it took lots of time. The two were gradually separated from each other's sight for longer periods of time until they were able to be permanently separated at different farms. This works for humans as well!

To prevent feelings of abandonment, provide reassurance to your children. Let them know where you are going and when you will return. If you are going on a trip without them, give them something of yours to look after while you are gone. To help them feel important and needed, assign them special chores or tasks like Mongo and Clyde had the special job at Camp Bearable. Let them know they are loved.

Sometimes we need a "transitional object"' to help us remember that loved ones still exist even when they are not around. Until they can developmentally achieve internalization, children often use "security blankets", stuffed animals, or jewelry, as a physical representation of the loved object. Apache had none of these. By age five, the process of internalization should be achieved and children feel safe and secure enough to spend the night away from parents, go to school, or engage in imaginary play. The best "transitional object" to assure emotional safety and security is God's Word. It worked for Apache.

"And these words, which I command thee this day, shall be in thine heart: And thou shalt teach them diligently unto thy children, and shalt talk of them when thou sittest in thine house, and when thou walkest by the way, and when thou liest down, and when thou risest up. And thou shalt bind them for a sign upon thine hand, and they shall be as frontlets between thine eyes. And thou shalt write them upon the posts of thy house, and on thy gates." (Deuteronomy 6:6-9 KJV).

GRIEF

To accompany the Bedtime Stories

RESCUED HORSES, CAMP BEARABLE, TRUST, THE MEMORIAL SERVICE

Horses form bonds, and when a horse is no longer a part of the herd for whatever reason, the other horses grieve. They whinny and run around the pasture looking for their missing friend. Sometimes they stop eating and sometimes they start "acting-out" by becoming stubborn or withdrawn.

While grief affects us humans emotionally and can affect us physically, grief primarily affects us spiritually. Grieving is a normal, healthy, positive process. As a process, grief has several stages. Children grieve differently from adults but they still go through stages. The first is typically shock shortly followed by denial. It is hard to believe that a beloved pet or loved one no longer exists. Once the loss is realized, sadness typically follows. Depression suggests prolonged grieving. Acceptance of the loss must happen to adapt and move forward with life. But children have many questions about death. When my nephews were small, the family dog got run over and died. My brother buried the dog before the boys could see the mangled body of their beloved pet. Out of curiosity, the boys dug up the dog to see it. They were sad but not afraid, just curious. My brother and sister-in-law were amused. Boys will be boys.

If your child has a concept of life after death, grieving is somewhat easier. Such a belief provides a sense of hope. Otherwise, a person may become "stuck" at some stage of grief. In the story "Trust", the horse Caio was "stuck". He had so many losses, he no longer trusted. He lost his identity, and his ability to connect with others was damaged. His "spirit" was broken. Some type of spiritual belief system is important for everyone, but especially for children. This is why Camp Bearable was formed.

As human beings, we are mental, physical, emotional, social, sexual, and spiritual all at the same time. Each aspect of our being must be addressed and "fed" or else we experience problems. Many parents are excellent in attending to a child's physical and mental needs but fail to acknowledge spiritual needs. When this happens, such a child may experience high anxiety, develop obsessive-compulsive behaviors, and lack emotional security. Therefore, experiencing a significant loss can be devastating. Depression and anger also accompany the grief process. Conflict with others, emotional outbursts, and social withdrawal are likely at some point along the way in grieving. Children may act out or become shy. Regression is typical such as reverting to sucking a thumb or bedwetting. In any event, allow your child to grieve. Don't get angry. Be patient and understanding. Give children the words to help them express what they are feeling. Model healthy grieving yourself. Talk about the loss. Don't try to replace the loss by going out and getting a new puppy to replace the old one. Allow time to grieve.

One of the best exercises to cope with grief is to write a letter to the lost loved one or pet. In this letter write everything you want the lost person to know-- feelings, confessions, thankfulness, etc. Then read the letter out loud and tear it up, burn it, or tie it to a balloon and let it go. Some type of ritual like the release of balloons or a service like in the story "The Memorial Service" can help to provide closure. It is often a mistake to "protect" children by not allowing them to attend a funeral service of a loved one. Closure is needed to move forward and develop new relationships.

Clyde and Mongo overcame their grief by becoming the Camp Bearable horses. They had new meaning and purpose in their lives. They had new friends and owners that loved them and cared for them. Just as Mongo and Clyde gained new identities, we may need to redefine ourselves to overcome our grief when we experience a loss that affects our identity. (See what happened to the horses in the story "Retirement").

"God is our refuge and strength, always ready to help in times of trouble" (Psalm 46:1 NLV).

DIVORCE

To accompany the Bedtime Story MAJESTY and LEADING FROM BEHIND

Hopefully your children will not have to directly contend with divorce, but some of their peers likely will. Even if divorce is in the context of friendship, your child may experience many of the feelings their friends are going through. Divorce causes feelings of anxiety, anger, sadness, grief, guilt, and blame. Children tend to blame themselves and feel at fault for their parents' divorce. Adolescents get angry at parents for not working things out that result in lifestyle changes, moving to another city or school, being deprived of love and relationship. If divorce is due to an affair, children feel abandoned and often feel they weren't good enough or loved because a parent left to live with another family. Respect is seriously damaged when divorce occurs. If respect is damaged, so are trust and obedience; therefore, acting-out and regression are common in children of divorce.

As a parent, it is important to understand that your child is going through a grief process when divorce happens. As previously stated, grief involves several stages. Recognize these stages and help your child understand what they are feeling by listening to them and being with them. You may feel guilty for not spending as much time with your child, just as Maggie felt guilty about not spending as much time with her horse Majesty. Don't make the mistake of throwing money and presents at them trying to buy back their love and respect.

Don't force another family on your children or yourself too soon. All too often after divorce, parents remarry trying to replace a mate and this can be a catastrophe. You are not just marrying a person, you are marrying a family. Put yourself in your children's shoes. Be patient and give them and yourself time to adjust to the loss of the original family structure. Each time a new horse came to the Equestrian Therapy Center, they had to be introduced to the herd. This was a gradual process. Pasture mates were carefully chosen based on their personalities. In family therapy with divorced parents, I always recommended remaining single until the children were out of high school.

It was blending a family too soon that necessitated the need for therapy in the story "Leading From Behind". The parents thought their love for each other was enough, but it wasn't. Give yourself time and allow God to lead the process of finding a new mate. As wise old Skeeter said in "The Beginning", "Well, I think God has a bigger plan for us all."

The best gift you can give your child is to love their other parent, even if divorce occurs. Reassure them of your love by being their parent. Don't try to become their best friend. Maintain appropriate boundaries but show them love and respect their feelings as you want them to respect yours.

Majesty became Maggie's best friend because he "listened". He was not judgmental, he didn't talk back, he didn't offer advice; he was just "with" her, and he allowed her to "be".

BULLYING

A major problem in schools today is bullying. On the prayer chain this week was a request for prayer for the family of a 15-year-old boy who had taken his life because he could no longer take the bullying he received at school. The following story was not in the book BEDTIME STORIES FROM THE BARN, nor was it in MORE BEDTIME STORIES FROM THE BARN. The story, however, combines many of the topics addressed in the PARENETAL GUIDE, such as depression, grief, divorce, and anxiety, which often contribute to bullying.

KICKBALL

"Boy, that was fun!" shouted JR as he pranced into his stall.

"Yeah, that was fun!" said Saint.

"Did we win?" asked JR.

"I think everybody won," responded Roanie. "Aunt Bev sets up the games so that everyone is a winner."

The afternoon's activity was kickball. Mr. Lee arranged three bases and a home plate in a diamond design like in softball. Each child was paired with a horse as a team. The object of the game was for each child to kick the ball into the playing field; then they were to run around the bases while leading their horse from home plate before being tagged out by the counselors. Mr. Lee rolled the ball from the middle of the playing field to each team of child and horse.

"My partner was the fastest runner, so we never got tagged out; we made three homeruns!" boasted JR. "So I should be the winner."

"My partner was a good runner but I'm not," said Prince sadly. His runner had been tagged trying to drag Prince around the bases.

Wise old Skeeter chimed in, "My partner is crippled and can't run, but I enjoyed trying to help her get around the bases."

"I was afraid I would trip over my partner, Julia. She kept stepping in front of me. I had to slow down, so we got tagged!" explained Clint, who was so much bigger than his little partner Julia.

"Cloe and I really worked together well as a team," said Saint.

"So did Ann and I," responded Roanie.

"It seems like the kickball game helped some of the boys and girls overcome their fear of us and boost their confidence," said wise old Skeeter.

"Yeah, I know what you mean," responded Roanie. "That new boy didn't want to participate at first, but when he saw how much fun the other kids were having, he joined right in. It looked like he had the most fun of all."

"I think you're right, Roanie," said Clint. "I overheard Aunt Bev say that this boy has few friends. He's bullied at school and now he is bullying younger kids in his neighborhood. That's why he's here; to try to learn how to get along with others."

"Most bullies suffer from low self-esteem and anger because they feel powerless to stand up properly for themselves," said wise old Skeeter.

"I didn't know the new boy had those kinds of problems," said JR. "We worked together as a team. I'm glad he had a different experience with us. He was not mean to me. We cooperated, so we should be the winners!"

"You may have had the fastest partner, but I'm the fastest horse," said Clyde. "I used to be a barrel racer!"

"Well, those days are long gone," said Saint. "Why did you get tagged out?"

"If I ran faster than my partner, I would have dragged him down. I wouldn't want to hurt him or run off and leave him. That's what bullies do. We were a team, so we stuck together. We did get to second base; we just got tagged out running to third. The whole point of this game was to work together as a team without grumbling or fighting, not necessarily to score points."

"That's the right attitude Clyde," responded wise old Skeeter. "It is not about intimidating, showing off, or threatening others. It's about working together in harmony and following the rules. That's what really makes you a winner."

"It's a bummer that there is no winner. I still think I should be the winner," complained JR.

"Did today's activity remind you of a Bible verse?" Roanie asked Skeeter.

"As a matter of fact, it did," replied Skeeter. "Don't count on your warhorse to give you victory—for all its strength, it cannot save you. But the Lord watches over those who fear him, those who rely on His unfailing love" (Psalm 33:17-18).

"Whether we're horses or humans, we are to rely on God's unfailing love, not our own strength to be real winners," said Skeeter.

"Amen to that," responded Roanie.

"Yeah, AMEN to that," replied all the other horses.

To prevent your child from being a bully, firstly, don't be a bully yourself. Refrain from any form or domestic violence including verbal abuse and harassment. The child's father in the "Kickball" story was a bully himself to his wife and son. Secondly, boost your child's self-esteem by engaging him in activities he can do and offer praise. Let your children excel at what they are good at, not at what you want them to be or learn (read about Caio in the story "Trust"). Then move on to more complex activities. Get to know your children as individuals by spending time with them one on one. If Aunt Bev had become what her parents wanted, she would have been a math teacher instead of a psychologist. God's plan always has a bigger purpose beyond what we can imagine. Offer three positives for every negative. Be positive and encouraging. Show love. Don't be so competitive. Teach your child to put himself in the other person's shoes to learn empathy.

"Make me truly happy by agreeing wholeheartedly with each other, loving one another, and working together with one mind and purpose. Don't be selfish; don't try to impress others. Be humble, thinking of others as better than yourselves. Don't look out only for your own interests, but take an interest in others, too. You must have the same attitude that Christ Jesus had" (Philippians 2:2-5).

Wise old Skeeter may have said it best in the story "Horses and Me Horse Show", I think what made today fun and successful is that we all behaved and worked together instead of focusing on competing." This truly is the best way to prevent bullying.

OBEDIENCE

To accompany the Bedtime Stories

A NEW TRAINER and THE COWBOY

"Children obey your parents in the Lord: for this is right" (Ephesians 6:1).

"Honor thy father and thy mother: that thy days may be long upon the land which the Lord thy God giveth thee" (Exodus 20:12 KJV). This is the first commandment with a promise. Honor, respect, and obedience to parents are important to God; so much so that it is one of the 10 Commandments. "Behold, I set before you this day a blessing and a curse; a blessing if ye obey the commandments of the lord your God, which I command you this day; and a curse, if ye will not obey the commandments of the Lord your God, but turn aside out of the way which I command you this day" (Deuteronomy 11:25-28 KJV). "What is more pleasing to the Lord: your burnt offerings and sacrifices or your obedience to his voice? Listen! Obedience is better than sacrifice, and submission is better than offerings. Rebellion is as sinful as witchcraft and stubbornness as bad as worshipping idols" (I Samuel 15:22 & 23 NLT).

Good things come when we are obedient, but bad things happen with disobedience. When the horses do what is asked of them, they receive treats. When they do not obey commands, they get a little whip or nudge with spurs, as the new trainer did in the story "A New Trainer". Not so much as to hurt them, but enough to get their attention. God has ordained contingencies. Rewarding children for obedience and behavioral compliance is not bribing. It is shaping good behavior and showing love, just like our Heavenly Father does with us when we are obedient and follow his Word.

Children are going to be disobedient—it is in our nature. Remember Adam and Eve? So how do I get my child to obey?—by using various forms of conditioning. In today's society, positive reinforcement has become the most effective technique to train children and animals. If you want your child to mind you, give them a reward for complying with your request the first time you ask. A reward is something that increases the frequency of a behavior. This is why treats are often used in training animals. JR has become conditioned to behaving when saddled because he knows that he will get a treat at the end of the ride. My nephew uses the potty because he knows he will get an M & M. Giving me a peanut butter sandwich for picking up my toys when asked would not be a reward for me because I do not care for peanut butter. But for some children, this would be a great reward. For food to work as a reinforcer your child needs to be hungry and it must be something they really like!

Keep in mind your child's age and stage of development. Give simple, clear, one step commands to small children, such as "put the truck in the toy box." That command is easier to follow and not as overwhelming as "pick up your toys." As the child matures, generalization develops and "pick up your toys" becomes sufficient to get the job done. Have realistic expectations of what you are asking your child to do for his developmental level. Behavioral charts are great and three-year-olds will work for stickers, but for older children, the stickers or stars must be paired with something tangible for them to work as a reward. A six-year-old may be able to wait to the end of the week to "cash in" their points for a prize at the dollar store, but a three-year-old needs a more immediate reward.

Punishment also works to get children to obey. There are two forms of punishment. One is the application of something negative such as a spanking. The other is taking away something positive such as taking away their cell phone. When done correctly and consistently, time-out can be effective because it combines both forms of punishment in that it removes the child from the rewarding environment and places them in a negative situation of isolation. If punishment is done correctly, there will be a decrease in the frequency of the undesirable behavior. Be consistent with whatever you do.

Obedience is to listen and apply instruction. Hearing is not enough. Following instruction is essential. "That's what God wants from all of us," said wise old Skeeter in the story "The Cowboy". "He wants us to be obedient and submit to His will for our lives."

"Mind your manners and respect your elders", Shiloh reminded Apache in the story "A New Trainer". "When you show respect, listen, learn to follow instructions, and do what you are told to do when asked, you then get special treats." Be sure to read this story to your children!

"The punishment of thine iniquity is accomplished" (Lamentations 4:22a).

DISABILITY

To accompany the Bedtime Stories

SPECIAL TREATMENT, THE JOCKEY, THE RAMP, HELPING HANDS, SPEECHLESS, CARRIE'S BIRTHDAY, THE OBSTACLE COURSE

In the story "Carrie's Birthday", the children who attended the party all knew Carrie from school. They were familiar with her limp and speech impediment, so they didn't tease or withdraw from her. They were her friends. Everyone encounters people with disabilities at some time. The first time your child sees someone in a wheelchair may be out shopping. Of course the natural inclination is to stare. Instead of withdrawing from the situation, approach carefully and courteously, teaching your child that people in wheelchairs are, unfortunately, a natural part of life for some. Show respect for the disabled person and model acceptance for your child. That's what Carrie's friends had learned to do.

Don't write off disabled people because they are different. The Jockey, when given the chance, regained his identity and joy. Find ways to include disabled friends and neighbors in your family's activities. Uncle Burt pushed the wheelchair for John in the story "Unity" so that he could participate in the team building exercises. The other church board members made a plan to go under the jump instead of over it to include John. Like in the story "The Ramp", my brother-in-law built a ramp for the steps to my house so that my father and his mother could attend Sunday dinner at my house in their wheelchairs. My brother bought a van so that he could transport my father and his wheelchair to church. My niece rolled her grandparents outside to sit in the sun instead of remaining inside for a visit. The Equestrian Therapy Center was famous for finding ways handicapped individuals could engage in normal activities like playing ball. One way was putting them on a horse and letting the horse be their legs. As in the story "The Obstacle Course", the horses at The Equestrian Therapy Center learned to behave and intuitively showed special care around the physically and emotionally handicapped. As Dude said in the story "Speechless", "We horses are able to help others when people can't."

Don't be afraid to include special needs children in your child's life. "Welcome them with Christian love and with great joy, and give them the honor that people like them deserve" (Philippians 2:29). Also, think about volunteering with special needs individuals at school or church or in the community, just like the men and youth from the church did in the story "The Ramp". Remember, "We are all precious in the sight of the Lord," said wise old Skeeter in the story "Entangled".

Read the story of Mephibosheth from the Bible, 2 Samuel 4:4; 9:1-13. Learn to treat special needs children like royalty—just like the horses did.

CARING AND COMPASSION

To accompany the Bedtime Stories

THIRST, A WINTER'S NIGHT, BIRTHDAY CELEBRATION, GENTLE SPIRIT, CARRIE'S BIRTHDAY, UNITY

A great example of caring and compassion is that shown by Skeeter toward Slick in the story "Thirst". Skeeter stayed behind to make sure Slick was okay when the other horses went out to see Aunt Bev and Uncle Burt in the swimming pool. Skeeter provided words of comfort and reassurance. He gave Slick hope, "Just think positively and believe and you will feel satisfied."

Uncle Burt showed compassion by partnering with his fellow church board member, John, who was in a wheelchair in the story "Unity". No one asked Uncle Burt to help John; he always lends a helping hand whenever there is someone in a wheelchair or using a walker. He shows genuine humility, caring, and compassion.

As Skeeter reminded the horses in the story "Carrie's Birthday", "We should treat the boys and girls that come to the Equestrian Therapy Center like royalty, not handicapped." This attitude should prevail. Be an example by modeling caring and compassion for others, like Uncle Burt. Teach your children to be kind and courteous. Teach them the Golden Rule: "Do unto others as you would have them do unto you." Have them imagine themselves in the other person's shoes and ask how they would like to be treated. This helps to develop empathy. Encourage your children to follow Dude's example in the story "Carrie's Birthday" when he said, "I promise to be nice and accepting."

Teach your children manners above and beyond "please" and "thank you".

Show kindness. Do something nice for someone else. Be a blessing.

FORGIVENESS

To accompany the Bedtime Stories

FORGIVENESS and CELL PHONE

Forgiveness does not mean that a situation is forgotten. Inappropriate behavior needs to be disciplined. Forgiveness does not mean "never having to say you're sorry" as in the movie LOVE STORY. Forgiveness means to let go of resentment. It means that once a situation has been disciplined, you go on as if the offense didn't happen. It has been pardoned.

We teach our children to say "I'm sorry", but it becomes a rote phrase instead of a meaningful expression of regret. God knows us and He knows our hearts. Forgiveness needs to be sincere.

Show forgiveness by trusting your child with something important again. "Get back on the horse!" Had Jack gotten back on Apache after he had been thrown off, Apache would have known that he had been forgiven in the story "Forgiveness". For example, my father gave me the car keys and let me drive the family car on the interstate highway on vacation not too long after I had driven the car out of town where I was not supposed to be going. Nancy came back to the barn and gave Skeeter treats after she got her new cell phone in the story "Cell Phone". Those gestures let me and Skeeter know that we were forgiven.

In the words of wise old Skeeter, "We should forgive in order to be forgiven. If you forgive those who do something to harm you, your Heavenly Father will forgive you, but if you refuse to forgive others, your Heavenly Father will not forgive you" (Matthew 6:14). So again, don't hold a grudge. Lack of forgiveness contributes to physical illness, depression and post traumatic stress disorder (PTSD). "But if we confess our sins to Him, He is just and faithful to forgive us and to cleanse us from all wickedness" (1John 1:9).

SUMMARY AND CONCLUSIONS

"Fathers, do not aggravate your children, or they will become discouraged" (Colossians 3:21); "rather, bring them up with the discipline and instruction that comes from the Lord" (Ephesians 6:4).

Why is the first topic in the Parental Guide on Anger Management? Why is the first scripture in the first topic "Provoke not your children to wrath"? Why is the closing verse "Father's don't aggravate your children"? It is because a child's nature is to provoke us and we overreact, thus, exacerbating the problem. Just as in training horses, parents must learn to discipline with patience and understanding instead of reacting or overreacting. Without consistent discipline, children can become dangerous, like the horse Apache.

By discipline I mean teaching, not just punishment. I like the Socratic Method of asking questions until a satisfactory answer with insight is achieved. I witnessed my niece do this with her five-year-old son this week. He hit his sister and she asked, "Would you want someone to do that to you?" This was followed by additional questions that led to what happened. In the end her son decided what his punishment should be. This method avoids a lot of unnecessary emotion.

The goal of parenting is to raise a responsible, independent adult. Parenting is our most difficult task and it is the one we are least trained to do. No instruction manual is included in the basket of items the hospital gives parents when they leave the hospital with a new baby. Hopefully, this Parental Guide has provided some insight, instruction, and encouragement to parenting in a simple and humorous way. Always remember that you are not alone in the parenting process. Ask for help. Seek wise counsel. Watch horse training videos. Include your children in your everyday activities. Read the Bible and pray with your family daily. Have fun. Love them. "Think of ways to motivate one another to acts of love and good works. . . . encourage one another" (Hebrews 10 24-25).

GLOSSARY OF HORSE TERMS

New World Dictionary of the American Language, Second College Edition

ANVIL—an iron or steel block on which metal objects are hammered into shape.

APPALOOSA—a breed of Western saddle horses with black and white spots, similar to a Dalmatian dog.

BAND—to encircle small sections of hair from a horse's mane with special rubber bands to form a series of "pony tails" that keep the mane in place for showing in a horse show.

BIT—the metal mouthpiece of a bridle used to control a horse.

BLANKET— the process of putting a large, thick, cloth covering on an animal to keep it warm.

BRIDLE—leather straps and metal pieces that form a headpiece for a horse so that he can be caught and guided.

CHAPS—leather fringed pants without a seat that are worn over jeans to protect a rider's legs.

CUTTING AND WORKING COW HORSE—specially bred horses trained to separate cattle from a herd.

DISMOUNT—to get off or down from the horse.

DOUBLOONS—worthless metal coins thrown to the crowds at Mardi Gras parades.

EGG-BAR SHOES—a type of horseshoe that is closed all the way around instead of in a U shape.

ENGLISH RIDING TACK—light weight saddles without a horn that are used in polo and fox hunting.

EQUESTRIAN—having to do with horses or horsemanship.

EQUINE—a horse

FARRIER—a person, like a blacksmith, who puts horse shoes on horses.

FOAL—a newly born horse or to give birth to a horse.

FORGE—like a furnace where metal is heated and hammered into shape.

GELDING—a castrated male horse.

GROOM—to brush and tend to horses.

HALTER—a rope or leather strap that goes around a horse's head so it can be tied or led.

HUNTER-JUMPER—usually a Thoroughbred horse that is trained to jump over obstacles. These horses are also used in fox hunting.

JAMBALAYA—people in South Louisiana typically cook this dish of rice, chicken, and pork in a big black pot to which is added a variety of vegetables and spices all "jumbled" up together.

JODHPURS—riding breeches made loose and full above the knees and tight from the knees to the ankles or a riding boot that is high enough to cover the ankle and calf of the leg.

LINIMENT—a medicated liquid that is rubbed on the skin for soothing sore or sprained muscles.

MOUNTING BLOCK—something like a set of steps that serves as a support when getting on a horse.

PADDOCK—a fenced field located near a stable where horses are kept.

PAINT PONIES—horses with multiple patches of white, black, or brown over their bodies.

PALOMINO—a cream, golden, or light chestnut horse that has a silvery white or ivory mane and tail.

PAVILLION—an open, ornamental building that is used for entertaining.

QUARTER HORSE—an American breed of horse characterized by a low, compact, muscular body and great sprinting speed for distances up to a quarter of a mile.

REINS—leather straps attached to the bit of a bridle used to guide a horse.

ROUND PEN—a round enclosure, usually consisting of metal panels, in which horses are trained.

SADDLE HORN—the top of a Western saddle that is to hold ropes for roping cattle. Most of the time it is used by people to hold on to the saddle while riding.

SHOD—to trim a horses hooves and put horse shoes on a horse.

SHOOT—a small enclosure from which a horse or cattle are run one at a time.

STABLE—a building where animals are kept. STABLED—to put animals in a stable for the night.

TACK ROOM—a room in a barn or stable where horse equipment like bridles and saddles are kept.

THOROUGHBRED—a purebred, well-trained, first-rate horse.

WITHERS—the highest part of the back of a horse located between the shoulder blades.

WRANGLED—to herd livestock, especially horses.

Printed in the United States
by Baker & Taylor Publisher Services